Winnie
AND Wilbur

WINNIE'S
Big Catch

's Parmar

The Shopkeeper

Big Doris

Stinky Stan

For Luka Duval – K.P.
For Katie Goodhart, with love – xx

OXFORD
UNIVERSITY PRESS

Great Clarendon Street, Oxford OX2 6DP

Oxford University Press is a department of the University of Oxford.
It furthers the University's objective of excellence in research, scholarship,
and education by publishing worldwide. Oxford is a registered trade mark of
Oxford University Press in the UK and in certain other countries

Text © Oxford University Press 2009
Illustrations © Korky Paul 2009
The characters in this work are the original creation of Valerie Thomas
who retains copyright in the characters.

The moral rights of the author/illustrator have been asserted

Database right Oxford University Press (maker)

First published in 2009
This edition first published in 2016

British Library Cataloguing in Publication Data
Data available

ISBN: 978-0-19-274837-9 (paperback)

2 4 6 8 10 9 7 5 3 1

Printed in Great Britain

Paper used in the production of this book is a natural,
recyclable product made from wood grown in sustainable forests.
The manufacturing process conforms to the environmental
regulations of the country of origin.

LAURA OWEN & KORKY PAUL

Winnie and Wilbur
WINNIE'S
Big Catch

OXFORD
UNIVERSITY PRESS

CONTENTS

WINNIE
Scores!

WINNIE'S
Big Catch

WINNIE'S
Knickers

Bump! **'Ouch!'** Swerve! 'Ow-ow-ow!
Don't do that, Broom!' wailed Winnie.

Winnie was on her way home from
shopping for groceries, riding her broom
over the treetops. But a wiffly wind and
having to dodge crows meant that it wasn't
a smooth ride.

'My bum's black and blue!' said Winnie.
'A knobbly bottom on a knobbly
broomstick is not a comfortable thing.'
She looked over her shoulder at Wilbur

who seemed perfectly happy. 'It's all right for you!' she said. 'You've got all that fur to pad you!'

Winnie went quiet as they landed. She didn't say a thing as they went into the house. Or when she dumped the shopping bags. She stood still and she stroked her chin and she said 'Hmmm' in various different tones—'Hmm, hmmm, hmmm?'

8

'Mrrrow?' asked Wilbur.

'I'm thinking,' said Winnie. 'Thinking
of a way to save my bum from getting
bruised.' She fell back into an armchair.
She waggled her bottom and bounced a
bit. 'That's it!' she said. 'I'll upholster
my bum!'

9

Winnie got out her rag bag and tipped rags onto the floor.

'Hmm. I need something soft next to my skin. Ooo, feel that, Wilbur! Bunny fluff. Lovely! Then something tough to protect me from the broom knobbles. How about this?' Winnie picked up a bit of rough canvas. 'But that won't look pretty. Hmm. I do like a pretty knicker.' She pulled out all sorts of fabric and chose the prettiest.

10

Winnie got her crocodile scissors and
cut out her knicker shapes. Then she tried
to thread a needle, but she couldn't
get the thread through the hole.

'Blooming heck!' said Winnie. 'I need
a bit of magic to help me with this.
Abracadabra!'

In an instant there was a squeaking and a squawking as a rat, a toad and some fleas set to work. The fleas hopped through the eyes of needles to thread them, while the others stitched. Winnie clasped her hands in delight.

'Oo, I can't wait to try the knickers on!'

The knickers fitted perfectly. Wilbur
put a paw over his mouth as Winnie looked
at herself in the mirror. 'Both pretty and
practical!' she said. 'Come on, Wilbur,
let's go for a test flight!'

13

The knickers made all the difference.
Even high in a thundercloud, with the
broom swerving this way and that,
bumping up and down, Winnie sat tight.

'Comfy as anything!' she said. 'Not a
bruise! Er . . . are you all right, Wilbur?'

But when they got back to the house,
Winnie started wagging her finger and
saying 'Hmmm' again. 'You know, Wilbur,
I really am a genius. These knickers are
easy-peasy fat slug-squeezy to make with
our little helpers. Let's make more of them
and set up a knicker shop!'

15

So they set to work making lots of
Winnie knickers.

'Put spider-web lace around the leg
holes,' said Winnie. 'Then we can charge
more. Now we just need a shop.' Winnie
waved her wand. 'Abracadabra!'

In an instant Winnie's front room had
turned into a shop. There was a big fine
till to put the money in. Winnie pressed a
button on the till. **Ker-ching!** it went,
and the drawer shot open, knocking
Wilbur off the counter.

'Mrrrow!'

16

'Whoops, sorry, Wilbur, but isn't it amazing! See all those compartments for the money to go in?'

They displayed the knickers in imaginative ways and put price labels on every pair.

'Open the door, now, Wilbur, and let our customers in,' said Winnie.

Wilbur heaved the front door open. **Creeeeeak!** . . . but there was nobody there.

'Oh,' said Winnie. 'Bother,' said Winnie. 'Mind you, I don't suppose anybody knows we're here. We'd better advertise. Write me a banner, Wilbur!'

So Winnie and Wilbur flew over the
village, trailing their banner.

Winnie's REINFORCED Knicker Emporium Now OPEN

'Quick!' said Winnie. 'We'd better get
back. There'll be a queue outside for sure
by now!'

But there wasn't a queue.

19

There was just Mrs Parmar.

'I could do with a pair of reinforced knickers because I'm going ice-skating and I'm bound to fall on my posterior from time to time, what with being a learner,' she said.

'These knickers would be just the job for that,' agreed Winnie. 'Now, what pattern would you care for? Ants pants?'

'Er . . . no. I don't think so,' said Mrs Parmar. 'Have you anything plain?'

'We've got a lovely plain black pair with lace trim.'

'Oh, I like those!' said Mrs Parmar.

'You won't mind if the odd spider is still working on the trim while you wear them, will you?' said Winnie.

'Er . . .' said Mrs Parmar. 'Perhaps I . . .'

'I'll tell you what,' said Winnie. 'Since you're my first customer, Mrs P, I'll do you a deal. I'll give you a complimentary frog to gobble up the spiders once they've finished, and then you won't be bothered by tickling in your knicker region.'

'Oh dear!' said Mrs Parmar, and she turned and ran out of the door.

'Strange woman,' said Winnie.  'Botherations! I want to use my till! Is anybody else waiting for a fitting, Wilbur?'

They weren't. Nobody else came to Winnie's knicker shop all afternoon.

'I'll just have to give my knickers away,' said Winnie sadly. 'I'll send a pair to each of my sisters. That'll be a nice surprise for them.'

So Winnie parcelled up a pair of these for Wanda.

And those for Wilma.

And them for Wendy.

'*Abracadabra!*' And the parcels were on their way.

'Right,' said Winnie. 'I'll keep seven pairs for myself. One for each day of the week. But that still leaves one pair left over. What shall I do with that?' She looked towards Wilbur.

'Mrrrow!' said Wilbur, and he began to run, but Winnie had him by the tail.

'Perfect for a cat hat!' she said, shoving the knickers over Wilbur's head. 'Two holes for your ears, and ever so pretty. Is it comfortable, Wilbur?'

'Hissss!'

24

'Oh, well,' said Winnie. 'I have got another idea. Just let me unpack those groceries.'

Winnie tipped packets of tea into her till; a different flavour tea for each drawer. Stinkwort tea, woodlouse tea, garlic tea, nettle tea, pea tea, fish-fin tea.

'Perfect!' she said. 'Each with its own place. Now I can be creative.' She shut the drawer. 'Hmmm. Which flavour shall I try? I think stinkwort and pea.' She looked at cross Wilbur. 'With a touch of fish-fin.'

Winnie pressed the buttons.

Ker-ching!

She spooned tea into the pot and poured on boiling puddle water.

'Now watch this!' said Winnie. She pulled the spare pair of knickers over the pot. 'A hole for the spout, and another for the handle. 'This tea's going to keep really warm. Am I a genius, or what?'

'Hmmeow,' said Wilbur.

28

Car Boot
WINNIE

'Where's the telly remote control, Wilbur? Have you been using it to play Cats In Space again?'

'Mrrow.' Wilbur shook his head.

Winnie picked up a jam pot with mould growing out of it. She picked up a hairnet and a stinky dish slop-mop and a torn pamphlet and a cracked cup with cold puddle tea in it. She lifted up her microwave and found dust and peas, a biro, a comb, and a nest of baby spiders.

She lifted up Wilbur's tail.

'Hiss!' went Wilbur.

'Sorry, Wilbur,' said Winnie. 'But I want to watch telly. Where is the blooming remote control?'

Winnie felt down the side of the sofa.
She pulled out a dirty sock, an old biscuit,
a very surprised mouse, and . . .

'Meeow!' said Wilbur, pointing a claw
at Winnie's cardigan pocket.

'Oh, I'm as silly as a dizzy flea!' said
Winnie. 'Well done, Wilbur. Sit down!'

Zap! On came Find Yourself In A Tidy House.

'A tidy house leads to a tidy mind,' said the smart presenter lady. 'Clear away your clutter! Get rid of your rubbish!'

'That's a good idea,' said Winnie. 'I might be able to find things if I didn't have so much rubbish. I'm going to tidy us up!'

Winnie began picking up leaky wellies
and rusty spanners and dirty plates and
broken nail-clippers and snail-squashers
and a fork with a bent prong. 'Now, where
shall I put all this lot?' asked Winnie. 'Er . . .
let me see . . . um . . . oh. We need a good
big cupboard, that's what we need.'

Winnie dropped everything on the floor.
'Come on, Wilbur,' she said.
'We're off to the shop.'

Winnie and Wilbur zoomed on her
broom down to the village furniture shop.

'I'll have that great big cupboard there,
please,' said Winnie to the shopkeeper.

'That'll be thirteen pounds then,
please,' said the shopkeeper.

'Thirteen!' said Winnie, tugging at her
hair. 'Pounds!' Winnie delved into her
pockets. She pulled out her toad-skin purse
and unzipped it. 'Er . . . will you take
twenty pence? And a fluffy toffee? And an
old blunder-bus ticket?'

'Thirteen pounds or nothing,' said the
shopkeeper.

'Oh, that's all right, then!' said Winnie.
'I'll have it for nothing, please!'

'No you won't,' said the shopkeeper, and
he began to push Winnie towards the door.

'Oh, *Abracadabra!*' said Winnie, waving
her wand.

Instantly there was a crisp new note of
paper money curled cosily in her purse.

'Here you are!' said Winnie, and she waved the note at the shopkeeper.

'I've never seen a note like that one before!' he said, frowning.

'It's a million-pound note,' said Winnie.

'A million pounds!!' said the shopkeeper. 'I haven't got change for that!'

'Keep the change,' said Winnie.

'Ha!' laughed the shopkeeper. 'Nobody would say "keep the change" for a *real* million-pound note! No, you can't fool me, Winnie the Witch. That's a forgery! Out of my shop, and don't come back until you've got some real money!' He hustled Winnie and Wilbur out through the shop door.

'That was as undignified as a rabbit with a shaved bottom!' said Winnie. 'How am I going to get enough normal money to buy that blooming cupboard?'

Wilbur pointed his tail at a poster. It showed cars parked in a field, and lots of tables with things on, and people looking at the things and smiling.

'Is it one of them car boot sale thingies?' said Winnie. 'Hey, that's a blooming idea! We can sell our things! You're doing well today, Wilbur!'

So Winnie packed up her rubbish.

'Hmm. We haven't got a car, so we haven't got a car boot,' said Winnie. 'We'll have to use the broom and carry everything in bags. We can still display things in boots if that's what they want.'

The poor broom struggled with the weight of Winnie and Wilbur and all those boxes and boots and bags.

'Come on, Broomy!' shouted Winnie.
'Up, hup! I'll comb your bristles for you
if you can get us to the school field!'

They landed with a **clatter-crump-crash!** Then set up their stall on the grass. A chipped potty, a broken slug trap, a blunt snake-slitter, a torn petticoat, a bust of Great Aunt Nelly with the nose knocked off, a bowl of gloop soup.

'Our stall looks as tempting as a tortoise teacake! You hold my hat for the money, Wilbur,' said Winnie. 'We'll soon be rich!'

But—**tick-tock**—the time passed and no money went into the hat, even though there were lots of people there. Wilbur put the hat on his head—**tick-tock**—Wilbur sat on the hat—**tick-tock**—Wilbur curled up and fell asleep on the hat.

Snore-purr, snore-purr.

Winnie propped her bottom on the broom and tried not to yawn. 'Why aren't they buying anything?' said Winnie. 'Look! They're buying all sorts of rubbish from all the other stalls. That's not fair!'

But nothing on the other stalls was quite as rubbishy as the rubbish that was on Winnie's stall.

Snorrrrrre! went Winnie, and she fell off her broom-prop. **Crash! Smash!**

'Ow!' Winnie had landed on the crockery corner of her stall, smashing it to bits.

'Meeow!' laughed Wilbur, waking up.

45

'Ha ha ha!' laughed the people at the car boot sale. They hurried over to Winnie's stall to see what was happening.

Winnie suddenly smiled. 'That's it!' she told Wilbur. 'This is our "lucky break!"'

'Mrrow?' said Wilbur.

Winnie got to her feet. 'Roll up!' she shouted. 'Just thirteen pence to throw a boot at the stall and see what you can smash!'

'Me first!'

'Then me! I want two goes!'

SMASH! CRASH! THUMP!
PING! SHATTER! SCRUNCH!

48

Soon Wilbur was staggering under the weight of money in the hat.

'We don't need that cupboard any more because we haven't got any rubbish left!' said Winnie. 'So what shall we do with all

49

this money? . . . Ooo, look at that! Just
what I need!'

Wilbur had his head in his paws, but
Winnie was pouncing on the next stall.
She'd seen a wand rack. 'Only thirteen
pence? I'll have it!' And some sloth
slippers. 'Ooo, I've always wanted some of
them!' And a cactus cat comb.

'Mrrrow!' said Wilbur.

'Yes, I'll have that too,' said Winnie.

It didn't take long before all the money in the hat was gone. And the pile of rubbish that Winnie and Wilbur flew home with was at least as big as the pile of rubbish they'd brought in the first place.

'You know what we need, Wilbur?' said Winnie. 'We need a cupboard to put all this lot in.'

Wilbur just sighed.

WINNIE

Scores!

Winnie and Wilbur were waiting to watch a football match at the village school.

'Meeow?' Wilbur pointed a claw at the basket Winnie was carrying.

'Oh, just a few snackaroos to keep us going,' said Winnie. 'I've brought pickled toad eggs, your favourite turkey tonsil tit-bits and a few sugared slow-worm tongues.'

Wilbur licked his lips.

'And I've brought . . .' went on Winnie.

But a small boy called Sam was tugging at
her sleeve. Sam pointed at Winnie's legs.

'You've got football socks on,' he said.

'They're not socks, they're stockings,'
said Winnie. 'And they're nothing to do
with football.'

'They're red and yellow, so you must
be in our team!' said Sam.

'I don't know how to play f—' began Winnie, but Sam wasn't listening. He was hauling her over to where the players were standing.

'See that other team?' said Sam. He pointed to the ones wearing purple and green socks. 'They're the Boggle-End Rovers.' Sam pointed to the biggest girl.

'That one's Big Doris. She's their captain. That's why we need a big girl too. We need you, Winnie.'

Winnie rolled up her sleeves. 'Righto,' she said. 'You just tell me how to play the game, and I'll do it.'

'Well, you must get the ball into the net to score,' said Sam.

'Easy-peasy, fat-slug squeezy!' said Winnie. She took out her wand. '*Abracadabra!*'

Instantly the ball shot from Sam's hands and into the net.

'Hooray!' said Winnie. 'We win!'

'No!' said Sam. 'You can't start until the whistle's blown!'

'Blooming heck,' said Winnie. 'Give me better instructions, Sam! What whistle? Let's get started! Come on, my little ordinaries!'

Brrrrip! went the whistle, and instantly Big Doris was kicking the ball, elbowing a boy, and stamping on Winnie's toes, all at the same time.

58

'Oooo, me bunions!' shrieked Winnie, hopping on one leg and clutching her ankle. 'You mouldy little cheat!' she shouted at Doris. But the Rovers had the ball and were passing it from one to another, zig-zagging towards where Sam stood in goal, his knees knocking together.

Pow! went the ball.

Leap! went Sam in the wrong direction.

Zap! went the ball, straight into the net.

'Goal!' shouted Doris.

Brrrrip! went the whistle, and they were off again. Thump, shove, trip, hit.

'Ow, ow, ow!' went Winnie's team. Kick, kick! went the Rovers.

'Goal! Ner-ner, we're the best. Their big captain's got a hairy chest! Two-nil to the Rovers! Eas-sey! Eas-sey!'

'Oh, kangaroos' poos!' said Winnie. 'Where's my wand, Wilbur? *Abracadabra!*'

Instantly the elastic was gone from the top of all the Boggle-End Rovers' shorts. And there was one long elastic between Winnie's leg and the ball.

Now Winnie was off down the field, kicking the ball. And every time a Rover, clutching his or her shorts, tried to reach the ball—**boing!**—the ball bounced straight back to Winnie's foot.

Kick-boing! Kick-boing!
Winnie was charging along, heading for goal. The village was cheering, 'Win-nie! Win-nie!'

Kick-boing, kick-boing went Winnie, nearer and nearer to the goal.

'You're the stinky cheat!' shouted Doris to Winnie. 'Ref! Ref! She's got the ball on elastic!'

But Mrs Parmar took no notice. Winnie was in front of the goal. She swung back her leg to give a mighty K I C K! The ball zapped straight towards the goal.

'Yes!' shouted the village . . .

. . . but just as the ball was about to cross the line.

BOING! it turned and **THUNK!** it hit Winnie right on her forehead, knocking her flat on her back.

'Mrrreeeow!' Wilbur rushed onto the pitch. 'Mrrow?'

'I'm seeing stars!' said Winnie in a dreamy voice. 'Stars and moons and rockets . . .'

The Rovers had the ball now.

'. . . and aliens and comets and . . .' went on Winnie.

Doris was heading towards the goal. She
ran past Wilbur and Winnie.

'. . . green monsters and galaxies . . .'
said Winnie.

'Silly old witch!' shouted Doris. 'Smelly
old cat!'

'WHAT?!' shouted Winnie, suddenly
awake and sitting up. 'What did you say
about my Wilbur?!'

Winnie was up on her feet. She ran fast
and she ran true. **Kick!** She kicked the ball
away from Doris. She swung her leg back
and gave the biggest **KICK** of her life
and . . . zapped the ball straight into the net!

'Goal!' shouted Winnie. She pulled her
dress over her head and ran around the field.
But only the Rovers were cheering.

Winnie put down her dress. She saw Wilbur shaking his head.

'But I scored!' said Winnie.

'You scored it at the wrong end and for the wrong team!' said Sam.

'Boo!' went the children.

'Boo who?' said Winnie. 'Me? Then I'll go and see to the refreshments. At least I can get that right!'

So Winnie set out her special snackaroos.

Brrrrip! went Mrs Parmar's whistle. 'Half time!'

The Boggle-End Rovers got to the food first. The village children didn't seem to mind.

Doris grabbed handfuls of the little scab patties. She dipped them into the mildew,

then stuffed them into her mouth.

'Yuck!' she said. **Spit!** Euch!'

'What? Don't you like them?' asked Winnie. 'Have a nice dribble smoothie to wash them down.'

Slurp! 'Euch!'

Now all the Rovers were all clutching their tummies.

Brrrrip! went Mrs Parmar's whistle. 'Second half! Erm . . . Winnie, please could you put the elastic back into their shorts?'

'S'pose so,' said Winnie. *'Abracadabra!'*

The two teams got ready to play.

'Don't worry if you lose, my little ordinaries!' shouted Winnie to the village team. 'I promise I'll cook a special tea for the losers!'

Sam looked at his team. 'We've *got* to win!'

70

Kick, dribble, dodge, kick!

'Goal!' the village school team scored, and again and again and again.

'Four all!' shouted Mrs Parmar.

'Tea for all the players if you draw!' said Winnie.

'Come *on*!' shouted Sam to his team.
He darted under the leg of Big Doris,
sneaked the ball sideways, ran forward,
and . . . **pow!** he kicked the ball into goal
so hard that it bulged the net and bounced
back to hit Doris on the bum.

Brrrrip! went the whistle. The game
was over.

'Yay!' shouted the village.

'Hooray!' shouted Winnie. But she told Sam, 'I did promise my tea to the losing side, so I'm afraid it will all have to be for the Rovers.'

'That's OK,' said Sam. 'Do you know, Winnie, you're as good at football as you are at cooking!'

'Am I?' said Winnie. 'Ooo, what a lovely thing to say, Sam.'

73

WINNIE'S
Big Catch

'Eh? What's this?' said Winnie, pointing to the calendar on the wall. There was a red scribble round and round the number 13, and arrows pointing at it. Winnie put a hand over her mouth. 'Of course!' she said. 'It's your blooming birthday, isn't it, Wilbur!'

'Mew,' said Wilbur sweetly, and he fluttered his eyebrow whiskers. He rubbed his head against Winnie and looked up into her eyes.

'I've not got you a present yet!' said
Winnie. 'And the thirteenth is tomorrow!
But I'll get something really good, Wilbur.
You stay here and comb your whiskers or
something while I go into my study and do
some internet shopping!'

With her tongue sticking out of her mouth to help her concentrate, Winnie slowly tapped the letters C-A-T into her computer, then clicked on the picture of a wrapped-up present. Up flashed pictures of cat food, cat flea powder, cat collars, cat worm pills, and cat litter trays. And that was all.

'Those are as dull as a snail telling you about the interior decoration of his house! Not very birthdayish, are they?' said Winnie to herself. 'And I've gone and promised Wilbur a really good present!'

Winnie clicked hard on the wrapped-up present picture again. Up came pictures of people doing adventurous things.

'Coo!' said Winnie. 'That's more like it! I could give Wilbur a special day, parachuting, or waterskiing, or sea fishing!' Winnie clapped her hands together. 'How exciting! Which shall I choose? Oo, it's got to be fishing. Wilbur does love his fish; jellied squeels and smackerel and octasquiggles, all that kind of thing.'

So Winnie clicked to book the fishing boat trip for the next day.

Wilbur didn't sleep a wink that night, worrying that Winnie hadn't got him anything. Winnie didn't sleep a wink either because she was bursting with wanting to tell Wilbur what his present was. So the moment the cockroaches squeaked 'cockroach-a-doodle-doo!' they both leapt out of bed.

'Happy birthday, Wilbur!' said Winnie. 'I'm taking you on a fishing trip out to sea for your birthday!'

'Meeeow!' said Wilbur, doing a claws-up, then dancing a quick jig, sailor-style.

'Waterproofs on!' said Winnie. 'Then we're off!'

They flew to the harbour, and found the boat owned by Stinky Stan the fisherman. It was called The Crabby Roger.

'Ahaaaa!' said Stinky Stan. 'Be you the woman and cat who think you'll be good at fishing?'

'Excuse me!' said Winnie, looking rather offended. 'Wilbur and I are both master fishermen!'

'Be you really?' said Stinky, tugging at his beard.

'Yes we do be,' said Winnie. 'So, start the engine and let's get going.'

'Mrrow?' said Wilbur.

The fishing boat was noisy and smelly.
It chugged through splashy waves
that got bigger and bigger.

Winnie held on to the side of the boat.
Wilbur was holding tight too.

'Ha haaa!' said the fisherman. 'I knew
you'd be useless at sea!'

Up and down went the boat. Up and down went Winnie's and Wilbur's tummies. Winnie had gone green. Wilbur's ears had gone flat.

'Not much of a treat so far, is it?' said Winnie.

'Blasted landlubbers!' said Stan.

'Blasted sealubber!' said Winnie.

Then the boat stopped. The sun came out, and so did the fishing rods.

'Now we'll have some fun!' said Winnie, cheering up. 'Let's catch some fish. Are you hungry, Wilbur?'

'Meeow!'

'Me too!'

'Bait yer 'ooks then,' said Stinky Stan.

Winnie and Wilbur fiddled with their hooks, attaching wriggling maggots.

'Seems a waste to feed them all to the fish!' said Winnie, popping one in her mouth. They cast their lines and waited . . . and waited . . . and waited.

'Hee hee,' laughed Stinky Stan, pulling up flipping fish after flapping fish.

Then Winnie felt a tug, and wound in her reel. 'I've got one! I've got . . . I've got . . . er . . . an old oil drum,' she said. 'Blooming heck!'

'Meeow!'

'Oo, Wilbur, what have you got? Reel it in! Up, up! . . . Oh dear.' Wilbur had caught some seaweed.

'I've got another!' shouted Winnie. 'Oh-oh! I can see it wriggling! It's alive! It's . . . it's . . . what the heck is one of them?' It was a very strange creature indeed.

'I knew you'd be rubbish at fishing!'
said Stinky. 'Look what I've caught!' He'd
got a whole basket of beautiful, shiny,
sensible-looking fish.

'We'll eat those, then,' said Winnie.

'Not blooming likely!' said Stinky.

'Them's mine! You catch yer own big fish!'

'All right, we will!' said Winnie. She whipped out her wand. *'Abracadabra!'*

And instantly, 'Mmrrrow!' said Wilbur excitedly. He'd got a bite on the end of his line.

'Hold on tight!' said Winnie, and she grabbed hold of Wilbur as something very big tugged at the other end. 'Heck, this one's huge!' said Winnie. Wilbur's fish began to rise up out of the water like a small island. It got bigger and bigger.

90

'It's a blooming whale!' shouted Stinky.
'Let go of your rod, cat, or it'll tip the
boat over!'

But Wilbur and Winnie held on, and the boat began to move, tugged by the whale. The boat went faster, and faster until it was just skimming the water.

'We're waterskiing!' said Winnie. 'Yippee!'

'Meeow!' said happy Wilbur.

The whale pulled even faster!

'Meeeeeeeeeeow!' went Wilbur as suddenly Winnie's skirt caught the wind and lifted them both up into the air.

'We're parachuting!' shouted Winnie. 'Isn't this a real treat, Wilbur?'

'Come back!' said Stinky.

Winnie looked down and she saw how green Stinky was. 'Oh, all blooming right! *Abracadabra!*'

Instantly, the whale went, and Winnie and Wilbur floated back down onto the deck of the boat as it ran up the beach.

'Just in time for lunch!' said Winnie.

Winnie and Wilbur made the old oil drum into a barbecue. Stinky shivered and steamed beside it.

'Skewer some of those maggots onto sticks to make kebabs, Wilbur,' said Winnie. 'We can have a nice seaweed salad.' She brewed a goo stew out of the odd fishy thing and other bits and pieces.

'Er . . . I is hungry too,' said Stinky. 'But I can't fancy any of that.'

'We weren't offering you any of that,' said Winnie. 'You didn't offer us any of your fish.'

'Well,' said Stinky. 'Ahrrr. Maybe I was a bit hasty there. Um. Would you care to share them fish with me, after all?'

'I reckon we blooming would,' said Winnie. 'You be our guest, then it's a proper party as well as a good present! Happy birthday, Wilbur!'

95

Enjoy more magic moments with **Winnie** AND **Wilbur**